The Movie Storybook

Adapted by Catherine Hapka

Based on the Teleplay by Annie DeYoung

Based on the Story by David Morgasen and Annie DeYoung

Printed in the United States of America

First Edition

1 3 5 7 9 10 8 6 4 2

Library of Congress Control Number on file.

ISBN 978-1-4231-2288-3

For more Disney Press fun, visit www.disneybooks.com

Visit www.DisneyChannel.com

DISNEY PRESS

New York

Carter Mason lived with her dad in a small town in Louisiana. Her life was pretty quiet. She got up, worked at her dad's bait shop, and went to school hoping that someday her cute classmate Donny would notice she was alive.

One morning, Carter was behind the counter at the Bait Shack when someone set down a bag of worms. She looked up and her stomach flipped.

"Donny!" she blurted out. "Hey!"

Donny blinked. "Hey," he said. "Uh . . ."

"Carter," she said, reminding him.

"Right. How much?"

"No charge," Carter said. "Free bait in exchange for never having to take the bus again."

"Great," Donny said.

Carter followed <u>Donny</u> outside. She stopped when she saw his car. Chelsea Barnes, the most popular girl in school, was in the front seat. Her best friend, Brooke, was in the back with two dresses on the seat next to her.

"There's no room for me," Carter said.

"She's right. Brooke's already wrinkling my after-lunch outfit," Chelsea said.

"It's high school, Chelsea, not Vegas," Carter pointed out. "You don't need a costume change."

Chelsea looked at Carter's well-worn jeans and high-tops. "Right. But you might want to think about it."

Donny drove away as Carter watched. Just then, Carter's dad pulled up.

At least I won't have to take the bus, Carter thought.

Mr. Mason drove through town.

"I can't stand them—they're such princesses!" Carter said.

There was a beeping sound from the dashboard. Mr. Mason pushed a button, and an LCD screen popped up. Carter's dad was also a secret agent for the Princess Protection Program. He helped keep princesses out of danger.

"It's Mason," Carter's dad said as he put on a headset. "Yes, sir. No, sir. Right away."

"You're leaving again?" Carter asked.

"Two days, max," Mr. Mason said. "Just a routine op."

It never got any easier for Carter to see her dad leave on a mission. "Be careful, okay?" she said finally.

"Always," Mr. Mason promised.

Far away in the tiny nation of Costa Luna, another teenage girl was beginning her day. The only difference was that she was in a palace, and she was wearing a full-length gown.

"Her Royal Highness, Rosalinda Marie Montoya Fiore. Princesa de Costa Luna!" announced Dimitri, the royal guard.

Sixteen-year-old Princess Rosalinda walked into her throne room. The servants stopped working to applaud.

"Dimitri, my coronation is a month away," Rosalinda said. "Why do we have to practice now?"

"Because everything must be perfect!" Dimitri said.

A well-dressed man hurried over to them. "What a beautiful coronation dress you are wearing. Who, may I ask, designed it?"

Rosalinda smiled. "You did, Mr. Elegante."

On a balcony overhead, Mr. Mason and Rosalinda's mother, Sophia, stood out of sight. They watched as a man in a military uniform entered the throne room.

"So that's General Kane?" Mr. Mason asked quietly.

"Dictator of Costa Estrella," Sophia explained. "He has always felt our two countries should become one—under his rule. Now that my husband has passed away, only Rosalinda can become queen of Costa Luna."

Below, the archbishop picked up a crown.

WHOOSH! A sword pierced the crown.

"I, General Magnus Kane, declare myself *el presidente de la República de las Costas!*" he shouted.

A group of soldiers surrounded the princess. Mr. Mason grabbed a rope tied to the wall and swung across the throne room. He landed beside Rosalinda. Sophia appeared and told them to run.

Rosalinda followed Mr. Mason out the door, as Sophia slipped away unnoticed.

Quickly, Mr. Mason led Rosalinda through a hallway and into a courtyard. They ran through the palace grounds. When their pursuers were far behind them, they stopped. Soon, Sophia stepped into view.

"Mamá!" Rosalinda cried. "Are you all right?"

"Yes, my darling. I knew General Kane would try something like this, so I made a plan to protect you." Sophia gestured to Mr. Mason. "You must trust Major Mason and do everything he says. Do you promise me you will do that?"

"Yes, Mamá," Rosalinda said. "I promise."

Mr. Mason heard footsteps in the distance. "We need to move."

Rosalinda realized her mother wasn't coming with them.

"The general will say you abandoned your country," Sophia explained. "I must stay so the people know you will return when it is safe." She fastened a gold locket around her daughter's neck. "Do not worry. We will be together again soon."

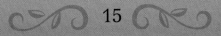

After Mr. Mason and Rosalinda escaped from the palace, a helicopter took them to a remote tropical island. Mr. Mason led the princess through a jungle to a concealed door. It slid open, and they entered a small, dark room.

"Princess Rosalinda," a woman's voice said, her image appearing on the wall. "You are now in the safe custody of the P.P.P., the international Princess Protection Program."

"You'll be safe now, Princess," Mr. Mason said.

Mr. Mason left. Rosalinda wished he hadn't. Her mother had told her to trust him, and she did. Rosalinda wasn't sure about anyone else.

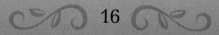

"Come inside, and I'll explain everything," the director said.

The wall opened. Staff sat at computers in front of a wall <u>covered</u> with flat-screen monitors. Some screens showed maps. Images of princesses were on others.

"Welcome, Rosalinda, to the heart of the Princess Protection Program," said the director. "A top secret agency funded by the world's royal families, we are actively providing protection services to twenty-nine princesses."

The director described several princesses the P.P.P. was protecting. The princesses had been sent to safe locations all over the world.

"What about me?" Rosalinda asked. "Where are you sending me?"

"Nowhere—yet," the director said.

A little while later, Rosalinda sat in the high-tech P.P.P. hair salon. A hairdresser approached.

"I want to speak with Major Mason," the princess said. Soon Mr. Mason appeared.

"Take me back to my country!" Rosalinda demanded.

Mr. Mason explained that Rosalinda couldn't go back as long as General Kane was in power. "You have to let us protect you."

"What about my mother? Who is protecting her?"

"As long as you're in Princess Protection, your mom will be safe," Mr. Mason said. "If you care about your country—and your mother—nobody can know who you really are."

Rosalinda knew she had no choice. "You may proceed," she said.

Soon, Rosalinda's makeover was complete. The director looked approvingly at Rosalinda's short, tousled hair, denim skirt, and simple silver earrings. "As of this moment, you are Rosie Gonzalez, an average American girl."

"What happens now?" the princess asked.

"Stage four: relocation," the director replied. "Somewhere General Kane will never think of looking."

Meanwhile, Carter had seen her father's jeep parked in front of their house, but she couldn't find him. When she got to her room, she saw a girl sitting on one of the beds.

"Who are you?" Carter asked the stranger, surprised.

"Rosa—uh . . . Rosie?" the girl said. "Major Mason gave me this room."

Carter stomped away in search of her father. She found him tying up a boat at the end of the pier.

"Who is she and why is she in my room?" Carter asked.

"I had to bring her here," Mr. Mason explained. "I'm going to need your help. She needs to blend in."

Carter refused. Then after her father gave her a pleading look, she sighed. "Fine. Who do I say she is?"

"Your cousin," Mr. Mason replied.

The next morning, Carter and Rosie arrived at school. As they got off the bus, they saw Ed, one of Carter's friends. Carter told him that Rosie was from Iowa. Then Rosie revealed that she had never heard of a homecoming dance.

"You're supposed to blend in!" Carter said to Rosie.

"I am trying," Rosie said.

"Try harder," said Carter.

In Costa Luna, General Kane was frustrated. He summoned
Sophia, who was his prisoner.

"Any news from Rosalinda?" he demanded.

Sophia was defiant. "No, and there never will be!"

Kane frowned. "Take her away!"

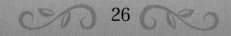

At school, Rosie's classmates weren't impressed that she already spoke French. Her other classes went a little better, but she was relieved when it was time for lunch.

Sitting alone, Rosie began eating her hamburger with a knife and fork. Carter sat down at Rosie's table.

"I thought you were going to blend in," Carter said.

Just then, the principal announced that one girl would be voted homecoming queen at the dance. Rosie was excited that everyone could vote. She nominated Carter! Embarrassed, Carter walked out of the cafeteria.

Carter was upset Rosie had humiliated her at school. So Carter tricked Rosie into doing her chores at the Bait Shack, starting with inventory.

"Inventory?" Rosie asked.

"Counting," Carter explained. "You count what's in here," she pointed to a jar full of night crawlers, "and put it in here."

Rosie carefully moved each worm from one jar to the other. When she tried to get a new jar off a shelf, the ladder tipped over. Wriggling worms, bugs, and little fish spilled across the floor and all over the poor princess.

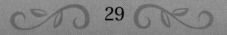

Carter and her father heard the crash and went to see what had happened. Rosie went to the cabin to change, and Mr. Mason and Carter cleaned up the shop. When they walked into the cabin, they saw Rosie standing by the table. It was set for dinner with a white tablecloth and candles.

"To thank you for cleaning up after the mess I made," Rosie explained.

They started to eat, but Carter didn't have much of an appetite. Mr. Mason kept complimenting Rosie on her homecooked meal.

"Must be nice to play peasant for a day," Carter said.

Rosie raced toward Carter's bedroom in tears. She wondered how she would ever fit in.

Carter realized she'd gone too far. She followed Rosie.

"My real name is Rosalinda Marie Montoya Fiore, and I am a royal princess," Rosie told Carter.

Rosie explained about her father's death and General Kane's attack. "We had to leave my mother behind," she continued. "Becoming Rosie Gonzalez was the only way to keep her safe."

Carter felt guilty for thinking of Rosie only as a princess. Carter realized she had been kind of hard on her.

"Let's just start over," Carter said.

"I only want to be a typical American teenager," Rosie said.

Carter smiled. "I think we can arrange that."

That evening, Carter took Rosie bowling. Some of their classmates were there, too. Rosie was surprisingly good. Ed, Donny, and the rest of the students were impressed. Chelsea and Brooke were not.

"The vote is on Monday," Chelsea said to Brooke. "We can't let her get more popular than we are."

Chelsea wanted to be homecoming queen. She came up with a plan to make Rosie think they wanted to be her friends.

Later that night, Rosie and Carter got ready for bed. "Shall we bowl again tomorrow?" Rosie asked.

"I have to work at the Bait Shack," Carter replied.

"I have never worked before," Rosie said. "I will help you."

"It's my job," Carter said. "You can't have everything that's mine!" Then she realized she wasn't being that helpful. "If you want a job, go get your own," Carter suggested.

"All right," Rosie said. "Good night, Carter."

Chelsea got Rosie a job at her father's frozen-yogurt shop. This was part of Chelsea's plan. She made sure a lot of their classmates were at the shop. Then she hit the self-clean button on the yogurt machine. Frozen yogurt poured all over Rosie.

But Rosie didn't get upset. "I am not a fool. She cannot make something of me that I am not," Rosie told Carter.

When Chelsea realized her prank had made Rosie more popular than ever, she was furious. Then Brooke pointed out that many people were talking about voting for Rosie for homecoming queen.

"No, I'm the queen!" Chelsea said. "We have to stop her." She and Brooke began to text their classmates.

That evening, Carter taught Rosie another skill: belching.

"If Mr. Elegante could see me now, he would be so mad!" Rosie exclaimed.

"Who's Mr. Elegante?" Carter asked.

"My royal dress designer," Rosie said. "If there were ever an emergency, he's the one I would call."

"Your own designer. Must be nice to be queen."

"It's not all about dresses and crowns, Carter," Rosie said. "To our people, my father was father, brother, and friend. I hope to be like him when I am queen of Costa Luna. I want to make a difference."

As they talked, Carter and Rosie realized they were becoming friends.

In Costa Luna, General Kane came up with a new plan: he would announce his engagement to Sophia. He thought this would make Rosalinda return home.

At school, Chelsea, Carter, and Rosie were nominated for homecoming queen. Then Donny asked Rosie to the dance!

Rosie said no, but Carter was still upset.

"You taught me how to act normal," Rosie said. "It is my turn to teach you. . . . Let's find your inner princess."

Rosie explained that being a princess was also about who you were inside, not just what you wore. Carter and Rosie offered tutoring to their classmates. They read to children at the library, and donated old clothes to a thrift shop.

At the shop, Rosie and Carter tried on lots of dresses and each found something to wear to the dance.

Later, they tried on the dresses again in Carter's room. Rosie had Carter practice walking with a book balanced on her head.

"I can't believe princesses actually have to do this," Carter said, walking slowly across the room.

"We don't," Rosie said.

"I hate you!" Carter exclaimed.

Rosie was startled. "You do?"

"I didn't mean 'I hate you' hate you. I meant, 'I hate you' like you're my best friend," Carter explained.

"I hate you, too. And that dress is ugly." Rosie smiled.

This time Carter was startled. "It is?"

"No, it is beautiful," Rosie said. "You are becoming a princess on the inside. Now you look like one, too."

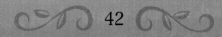

Meanwhile, Brooke was working on a homework assignment for Spanish class. She was flipping through a stack of Spanish-language gossip magazines. Suddenly, she saw a photo of a familiar face.

"Princess Rosalinda?" she murmured. "No way!"

That afternoon, Brooke and Chelsea went to Carter's house. They showed Rosie a magazine article about General Kane's engagement to Rosie's mother.

Chelsea and Brooke just wanted to win the homecoming crown. They didn't care what they had to do. As they left, they dropped Rosie's and Carter's dresses for the dance into a mud puddle.

Carter was furious when she saw the ruined dresses. She forgot about them when she realized Rosie was crying.

"I have to leave!" Rosie said, showing her the article.

Carter tried to change Rosie's mind, but she refused to listen. Carter knew if Rosie went back to Costa Luna, she'd end up a prisoner.

Carter remembered that Mr. Elegante, Rosie's dress designer, was the person Rosie would turn to in an emergency. Carter talked to Mr. Elegante, and they came up with a plan.

Later in Costa Luna, Mr. Elegante told General Kane that he had discovered the location of the princess and that she would be at the homecoming dance wearing a blue dress.

Carter convinced Rosie to go to the dance before she left. They did their hair and makeup. Then Carter pulled out one pink dress and one blue dress that Mr. Elegante had sent.

Carter also had masks for them to wear. She'd gotten enough for all their friends, too.

Carter, Rosie, and their friends arrived at homecoming wearing masks. Donny saw Carter and wanted to ask her to dance. Carter stopped him. She had realized that she deserved better.

Meanwhile, General Kane's helicopter landed behind the school. General Kane planned to capture Rosalinda and take control of Costa Luna once and for all.

Inside the school auditorium, Carter stayed near the door, wearing her mask. She looked around and saw General Kane. He saw her, too, and recognized the blue dress. He thought Carter was Rosalinda.

"Take her now!" General Kane said to his soldiers.

They grabbed Carter, shoving aside a couple of freshman boys. The soldiers led her outside, then toward the helicopter. Nobody else noticed the scuffle.

"Your mother will be pleased to see you, *Princesa*," General Kane said.

Carter knew better than to respond. If she spoke, he would realize she wasn't Rosalinda.

Inside the auditorium, the principal announced the votes for homecoming queen. "The winner is . . . Rosie Gonzalez!"

The students in the gym cheered loudly. Rosie walked onstage and thanked her classmates for electing her queen.

"I've learned about friendship and loyalty and trust," Rosie said. "I want to thank Carter Mason for teaching me this."

Rosie looked around the room for Carter. Just then, two freshman boys rushed over.

"These crazy-looking security dudes just took Carter away," one of them said.

For a moment, Rosie was confused. Then she guessed what had happened. She raced toward the door.

Rosie ran through the school grounds. Finally, she caught up to Carter and General Kane.

"This is my fight, not yours," Rosie said to Carter.

The general led Rosie toward the helicopter. As they walked up, the door opened to reveal Mr. Mason and other P.P.P. agents. Then even more agents surrounded General Kane and his men.

"We're turning you over to the international authorities," Mr. Mason said.

Rosie hurried over and hugged Carter. They were safe! "I cannot believe you did this all for me!" Rosie exclaimed.

"That's what princesses do, right?" Carter said.

"Yes," Rosie agreed. "And you are truly a princess."

Soon after, Rosie returned to Costa Luna. Carter and Mr. Mason went with her. They attended the princess's coronation.

"I present to you Queen Rosalinda Marie Montoya Fiore of Costa Luna," the archbishop said.

Everyone at the ceremony cheered loudly, including Carter.

Carter was happy she and Rosie had made a difference and helped each other. Plus, they had each gained a good friend!

TABLE OF CONTENTS

CHAPTER ONE
Scrambled Eggs
4

CHAPTER TWO
An American Mink's Life
7

CHAPTER THREE
How the Mink Invade
12

CHAPTER FOUR
What's the Problem?
18

CHAPTER FIVE
Working on Answers
24

Map
28

Glossary
30

For More Information
31

Index
32

About the Author
32

SCRAMBLED EGGS

An American mink mother cares for her six-week-old babies.

An American mink mother waddles along the lakeshore, and five little mink follow. It's evening, and the little mink are hungry. The mother hears the call of a gull and turns to look in its direction. The bird is running in an open space not far away. Its nest must be nearby. The mother mink goes to check it out, and her young ones follow close behind.

The gull spots the mink and is alarmed. She trots back and forth, and her cries grow louder. Then she spreads her wings and lifts into the air. She rises, turns, and dives toward the mink family. The mink crouch close to the ground. The bird swoops past, turns, and dives again.

Just then, the mother mink spots the gull's nest on the ground. Three eggs lie inside the nest. Again the mink hug the ground as the bird passes. Then they race for the nest. Within seconds, the mother and her babies are upon the eggs.

Learning & Innovation Skills

American mink are said to be an invasive species in many countries. An invasive species is a plant or animal that has moved into and taken over a new place. Invasive animals often have no natural enemies in their new homes. No animals hunt them to keep their numbers down. The invasive species population is able to grow out of control. What problems might this cause for other animals in the area?

With an American mink nearby, these
unattended goose eggs are in danger.

The gull cries loudly but is helpless. She dives again, this
time just grazing a little mink with her claws. But it's too
late. The mink wipe their faces with their tiny paws and
turn to head back to the lake.

CHAPTER TWO

AN AMERICAN MINK'S LIFE

The American mink has a white patch of fur on its chin.

The American mink is a mammal with thick, glossy, brown or black fur. It has a white- or cream-colored patch on the chin and sometimes on the throat. The mink has a long, slender body and short legs. Its tail is long and

An American mink makes its way across a wetland.

thick. These animals have dark eyes and small, round ears.
Their streamlined bodies are perfect for scurrying through
tunnels and squeezing through tight places.

Adult mink are about 17 to 28 inches (43 to 71
centimeters) long. They weigh about 1.3 to 3 pounds (0.6
to 1.4 kilograms). The males are much larger than the
females—usually twice as heavy!

These American mink make their den in a hollow log by a river.

American mink usually live very close to water. They can be found near lakes, streams, and rivers, as well as in swamplands and along coastlines.

A mink makes its home, or den, in any small, safe space it can find. Hollow trees, old rabbit burrows, or holes along a riverbank make excellent dens.

Learning & Innovation Skills

Quite often, mink kill more than they can eat at one time. This behavior is called surplus killing. Mink are not the only animals to engage in this activity. Foxes and coyotes are also thought to be surplus killers. An animal might kill more than it needs to feed its young. Can you think of another reason why an animal might overkill?

Female mink have their babies, or kits, in the late spring or summer. They usually have three to eight kits in a litter. The young stay with their mother for about three months, playing, exploring, and learning to hunt. Then they leave home and find dens for themselves. In the wild, most live only two or three years.

Mink are meat eaters. They hunt and kill many different kinds of prey. Sharp teeth and powerful jaws help the mink catch and eat their food. Mink feed on fish, rats, birds, crayfish, lizards, rabbits, muskrats, and other small animals. They also feed on the eggs of birds.

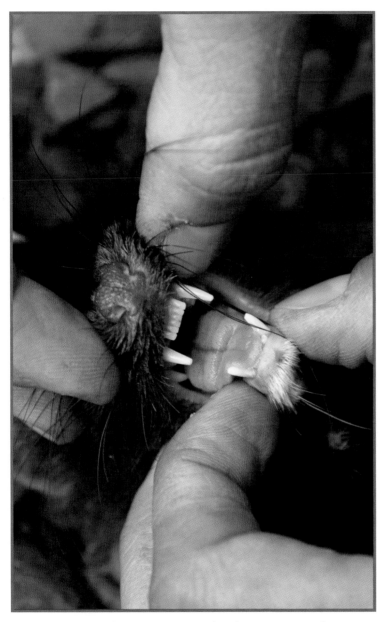

American mink belong to a family of mammals called the mustelids. The mustelid family includes American mink, European mink, European polecats, otters, weasels, ferrets, and badgers. Many of them are prized for their fur.

Mustelids have a scent gland near the base of the tail. The gland produces a very strong-smelling fluid. Mustelids use it to mark their territories. Why do you think an animal needs a territory?

A researcher examines a sedated American mink to determine its age. White teeth that aren't worn down suggest that the animal is not yet an adult.

CHAPTER THREE

HOW THE MINK INVADE

*The natural range of the American mink
covers large parts of North America.*

American mink are native to much of the United States and Canada. However, in the 20th century, they came to live in South America, Europe, and Asia. The American mink is now invading these lands. What happened?

Through much of the 20th century, warm clothing made out of American mink fur was very popular. People in North America and around the world wore mink coats, jackets, and hats. These items were often very expensive. The very best mink coats cost thousands of dollars.

In order to make mink coats and hats, clothing factories bought **pelts** from North American fur farmers. The farmers raised, fed, and eventually killed the animals for their fur. Healthy, well-fed mink with no scars made the best pelts. Their fur was shiny, soft, and thick. These fine furs brought

Invasive species are not always animals. Sometimes they are plants. People might put rare or unusual plants in their gardens—plants that came from other countries. But it may not take long for those plants to produce seeds and for the seeds to spread. This is often how invasive plants get started and then grow out of control.

Invasive plants might spread quickly and choke out other plants that have been there for years. In some cases, those other plants provided leaves or fruit for animals to eat. But an invasive plant can wipe out that food supply. In what other ways might invasive plants harm animals?

Breeding on mink farms has produced different fur colors, including white and silver for these mink hats.

the highest prices. In a good year, a mink farmer could earn quite a bit of money.

In the 1920s, other countries decided to start fur farms. They bought and raised American mink. By the 1930s, there were fur farms in France, Sweden, Norway, England,

Denmark, and Iceland. Farms sprang up in other European countries, in Russia, and even in Chile during the next few decades.

American mink on farms were not invasive. They did not run loose or prey on other animals. The trouble started when the mink did not *stay* on the farms.

It did not take long for some of these small, slender, and fast animals to escape. Almost as soon as people began setting up fur farms, mink began escaping into the wild. They zipped into burrows and found plenty of small spaces to hide. These mink had litters in the wild, and in time, their young spread out and had

litters of their own. Even with the losses, fur farming remained a good business.

Then, starting in the 1960s, things began to change. In some countries, the popularity of mink clothing dropped. People began wearing coats, jackets, and hats made of "fake fur." Fake fur is a factory-produced material that feels like real fur but is less expensive.

At about the same time, many people began to complain about fur farms. They did not like the idea of animals being killed to make clothing. Soon the fur business began to decline.

Over the next few years, many fur farms shut down. It was pointless to raise mink that no one would buy. Farmers could not afford to keep their animals, so many simply opened the cage doors and let their mink run free.

In Europe and Russia, thousands of American mink were released. Many died of hunger or thirst,

Farms around the world continue to raise and sell American mink. This mink farm is in Kazakhstan.

or they became prey to other animals. But many others made their way to lakes, rivers, and streams, where they found plenty of food and water. The weather, food supply, and abundance of hiding places were perfect. The mink increased, spread, and increased some more.

CHAPTER FOUR

WHAT'S THE PROBLEM?

Outside of North America, the American mink is driving out native species.

Today, the American mink is an invasive species in Europe, South America, and Russia. People call the animal a pest. Governments are paying people to get rid of them. Scientists are figuring out ways to move them out.

Landowners are working out methods to eliminate them. Even the people who protect wildlife wish they would disappear. What is it about these little, furry creatures that arouses such feelings?

Wherever American mink move in, some of the native species begin to disappear. The populations of European mink, small rodents, and shorebirds start to drop. In certain areas, the usual animal species have vanished altogether because of the American mink.

American mink and European mink live in the same kind of habitat. They both prefer to live near rivers, streams, lakes, and ponds. They both hunt and eat a wide variety of foods. They make their dens in small, safe cavities. But these two species of mink simply cannot live together.

Because American mink are larger, they eat more of the available food. They leave little for the European mink.

In large part because of the American mink, the European mink is beginning to disappear from its natural habitat.

The American mink are also more aggressive. American mink males will usually chase off European males and females from their territories.

Because they are often under attack, European mink have begun to disappear. Other factors, such as habitat destruction and pollution, are also harming the European mink. But the spread of the American mink has made the situation worse. The European mink is now in danger of becoming extinct.

Other animals are at risk because of the invasive American mink. One is the rat-sized water vole that lives throughout Great Britain and in parts of Europe and Russia. The water vole, like the mink, lives near lakes, creeks, and rivers. It spends much of its time in underground burrows. The vole feeds on grass, fruits, plant buds,

21st Century Content

American mink are not the only cause of some decreasing animal populations. Many animal populations were vanishing before the mink arrived. In many countries, the destruction of animal habitats has been going on for years. As cities have spread out, new houses and businesses have sprung up. Places that once were home to European mink, voles, and other animals have been turned into neighborhoods. Animals that once found safety along riverbanks now have to watch out for dogs and cats. Pollution has also been a problem. Chemicals from homes and factories have found their way into streams and rivers, where animals drink the unsafe water. What do you think we could do as local and global citizens to keep native wildlife from disappearing?

twigs, and roots. Foxes, owls, herons, even a freshwater fish called pike hunt the vole. Now American mink also hunt water voles.

Fortunately, the vole has ways to escape most enemies. When a fox or an owl threatens, the vole leaps into the water. When a heron or pike threatens, it races into its burrow. It has survived this way for many years. That is, until the American mink arrived.

The water vole's escape plans are useless against the American mink. When the vole jumps into the water, the mink goes right after it. When it runs into its burrow, the slender mink is right behind.

The water vole is facing the same problems as the European mink. Its habitat is being destroyed. But the appearance of the American mink has made matters worse. The water vole is disappearing rapidly in Great Britain, and in some places, it has vanished altogether.

American mink prey on eider ducks in Great Britain.

Birds that nest near water are also in danger. Eiders, oystercatchers, gulls, and terns build their nests on the ground. Eggs, young, and even adults guarding the nests can fall prey to American mink. Scientists have kept track of different ground-nesting birds in Scotland. They have seen their numbers dropping—again because of the American mink's feeding habits.

WORKING ON ANSWERS

*Controlling invasive species like the American mink
is a challenge for today and tomorrow.*

Today, many people are trying to find ways to control the American mink. It's not an easy task. It is difficult to find a method that reduces the mink numbers without harming other animals.

In some areas, people have tried trapping the mink. However, this is expensive and time-consuming. People have to make or buy the traps. They have to set them in areas where American mink live. And they have to

Trapping American mink is one way to reduce their unwanted populations.

check the traps at least every 24 hours. Sometimes the traps stay empty, and sometimes they catch European mink. Some regions may have hundreds or even thousands of American mink. Trapping in these places won't change the situation very much.

Scientists are wondering if otters might help control the mink. Otters live in the same habitats that American mink do. They like to be near water, just as mink do. They also eat the same foods that mink eat. But in Great Britain, the otters are about seven times bigger than American mink. In places where otter numbers are going up, the American mink numbers seem to be going down. Perhaps otters are killing the mink or running them off.

It is probably impossible to remove the American mink completely from countries they have invaded. Many people think that their best hope is to remove the animals from a few small areas at a time. Then fences or barriers could be built to keep the mink out.

Much work remains to be done on this problem. But scientists and wildlife experts are learning more and more all the time. Perhaps one day, they will learn the best way to deal with this furry invader.

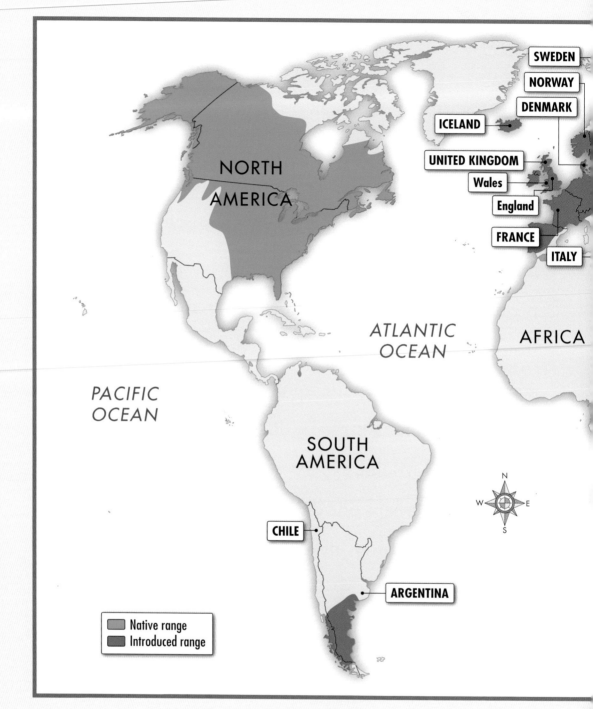

This map shows where in the world the American mink

21st CENTURY SKILLS LIBRARY

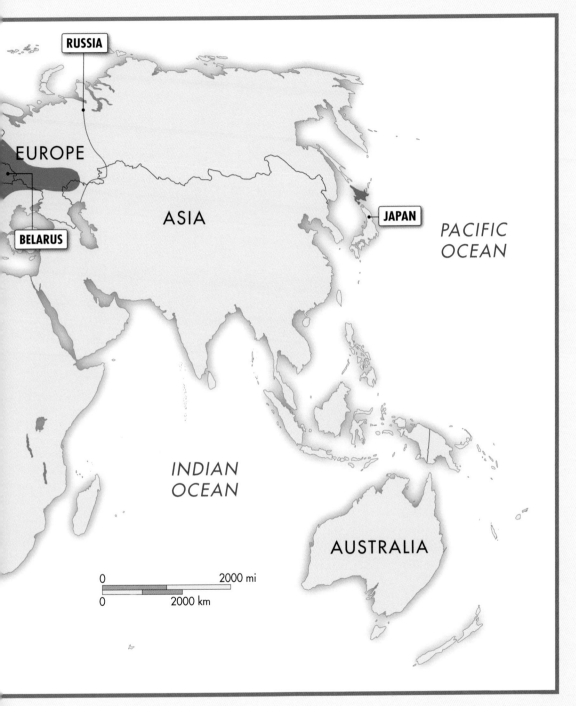

RUSSIA

EUROPE

BELARUS

ASIA

JAPAN

PACIFIC
OCEAN

INDIAN
OCEAN

AUSTRALIA

0   2000 mi

0   2000 km

lives naturally and where it has invaded.

GLOSSARY

extinct (ek-STINGT) completely died out

gland (GLAND) a body organ that produces a specific substance that is used or given off; glands make tears and sweat

habitat (HAB-ih-tat) the area where a plant or animal normally lives

litter (LIH-tur) all of the young born at one time to the same mother

mammal (MAM-uhl) a fur-bearing animal that has live young

mustelids (MUSS-tuh-lidz) a family of mammals that includes American mink, European mink, European polecats, otters, weasels, ferrets, and badgers

pelts (PELTS) the hides or skins of animals

prey (PRAY) animals that are eaten by other animals

rodents (RO-duhnts) mammals such as squirrels, mice, rats, and beavers that have large front teeth for gnawing

species (SPEE-sheez) a group of similar plants or animals

surplus killing (SUR-pluss KIL-ing) a behavior where an animal kills more than it can eat

territories (TEHR-ih-tor-eez) areas that animals defend as their own

For More Information

Books

Klobuchar, Lisa. *Badgers and Other Mustelids.*
Chicago: World Book, Inc., 2005.

May, Suellen. *Invasive Aquatic and Wetland Animals.*
New York: Chelsea House, 2007.

Morgan, Sally. *The Weasel Family.*
North Mankato, MN: Chrysalis Education, 2004.

Web Sites

American Mink—ARKive: Images of Life on Earth
www.arkive.org/species/ARK/mammals/Mustela_vison/
To see photographs and watch videos of the American mink

Derbyshire Wildlife Trust—Water Voles and Mink
www.derbyshirewildlifetrust.org.uk/index.php?section=watervole:mink
For details about the problems with mink and water voles

Global Invasive Species Database: *Mustela vison*
www.issg.org/database/species/ecology.asp?si=969&fr=1&sts=sss
For a description of the American mink

INDEX

animal-rights activists, 26

babies. *See* kits.
birds, 4–5, 6, 10, 19, 23
body, 8

clothing, 13, 16
colors, 7–8, 16

dens, 9, 10, 19

ears, 8
European mink, 11, 16, 19–21,
    22, 25
extinction, 21
eyes, 8

females, 9, 10, 20
food, 4–6, 10, 13, 15,
    17, 19, 22, 23, 26
fur, 7, 11, 13
fur farming, 13–15, 16–17, 26

generalists, 15
governments, 18, 26

habitats, 9, 10–11, 12, 19,
    20, 21, 22, 26, 28–29
humans, 13–15, 16–17,
    18–19, 21, 24, 25, 26, 27
hunting, 4–6, 10, 19, 22

invasive species, 5, 6, 13,
    15, 18, 21

kits, 4, 5, 6, 10, 16

legs, 8
length, 9
litters, 10, 15, 16

males, 9, 20
mustelid family, 11

native species, 12, 19–23

otters, 26

pelts, 13, 16
pollution, 20, 21
prey, 4–6, 10, 13, 15, 17, 19,
    22, 23, 26

rodents, 19

scent glands, 11
sizes, 9, 16, 19
specialists, 15

tails, 8
teeth, 10
territories, 11, 20
trapping, 25–26

water birds, 4–5, 6, 19, 23
water voles, 21–22
weight, 9

ABOUT THE AUTHOR

Susan H. Gray has a master's degree in zoology. She has written more than 70 science and reference books for children, and especially loves writing about animals. Gray also likes to garden and play the piano. She lives in Cabot, Arkansas, with her husband, Michael, and many pets.

21st
Century
Skills Library

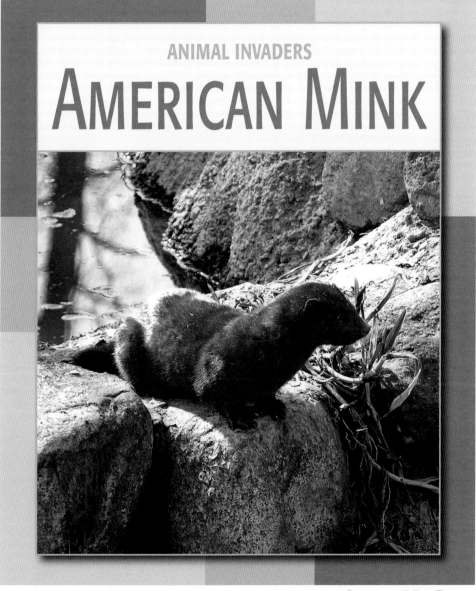

ANIMAL INVADERS

AMERICAN MINK

Susan H. Gray

Cherry Lake Publishing
Ann Arbor, Michigan

Published in the United States of America by Cherry Lake Publishing
Ann Arbor, MI
www.cherrylakepublishing.com

Content Adviser: Lauren A. Harrington, Wildlife Conservation Research Unit,
Department of Zoology, University of Oxford, Oxford, England

Please note: Our map is as up-to-date as possible at the time of publication.

Photo Credits: Cover and page 1, © Biopix.dk:JCSchou; page 4, © Erwin & Peggy Bauer/
Animals Animals; page 6, Courtesy of Elke Schüttler; pages 7, 8, 11, 12, and 24, Courtesy
of André Künzelmann/Helmholtz Centre for Environmental Research–UFZ; page 9, ©
iStockphoto.com/JohnPitcher; page 14, © iStockphoto.com/jeffulrich; page 17, © vario
images GmbH &Co.KG/Alamy; page 18, © Andrew Harrington/Alamy; page 20, © Niall
Benvie/Alamy; page 23, © iStockphoto.com/tirc83; page 25, © mammalpix/Alamy

Map by XNR Productions Inc.

Library of Congress Cataloging-in-Publication Data
Gray, Susan Heinrichs.
American mink / by Susan H. Gray.
    p. cm.—(Animal invaders)
Includes index.
ISBN-13: 978-1-60279-114-5
ISBN-10: 1-60279-114-7
1. American mink—Juvenile literature. I. Title. II. Series.
QL737.C25G735 2008
599.76'627—dc22   2007033721

*Cherry Lake Publishing would like to acknowledge the work of
The Partnership for 21st Century Skills.
Please visit* www.21stcenturyskills.org *for more information.*